The Day Gogo Went to Vote

South Africa, April 1994

by Elinor Batezat Sisulu

Illustrated by Sharon Wilson

 Little, Brown and Company

BOSTON NEW YORK TORONTO LONDON

This book is a tribute to our grandparents and great-grandparents,
who struggled all their lives for the right to vote.
May their patience and wisdom be a beacon for future generations.
— E. B. S.

To my mother
— S. W.

I would like to thank Mary Tiseo for her faith in me.
Without her, this book would not have been published.
Thanks as well to the Mokwena family for making the story come alive.
And I also thank Gcina Mhlophe for her encouragement and support
and for the fine example she sets to aspiring storytellers. — E. B. S.

Text copyright © 1996 by Elinor Batezat Sisulu
Illustrations copyright © 1996 by Sharon Wilson

First Edition

Library of Congress Cataloging-in-Publication Data
Sisulu, Elinor.
    The day Gogo went to vote / Elinor Batezat Sisulu ; illustrated by
Sharon Wilson. — 1st ed.
        p.   cm.
    Summary: Thembi and her beloved great-grandmother, who has not
left the house for many years, go together to vote on the momentous
day when black South Africans are allowed to vote for the first time.
    ISBN 0-316-70267-6
    1. Blacks — South Africa — Juvenile fiction. [1. Blacks — South
Africa — Fiction. 2. Voting — Fiction. 3. South Africa — Fiction.
4. Great-grandmothers — Fiction.] I. Wilson, Sharon R., ill. II. Title.
PZ7.S6225Day 1996
[E] — dc20   95-5300

10 9 8 7 6 5 4 3 2

NIL

Published simultaneously in Canada by Little, Brown & Company (Canada) Limited
and in Great Britain by Little, Brown and Company (UK) Limited

The artwork for this book was created with pastels on sanded board.

Printed in Italy

Glossary and Pronunciation Guide

Eleven different languages are spoken in South Africa. Many families and communities use a combination of different dialects in their everyday speech. The names and colloquial expressions used in this book are in Xhosa and Zulu, two of the major dialects spoken in Soweto, where this story takes place (though it could have happened in any of the many townships that make up South Africa).

gemmer [HEM-airr] (with a guttural *g* and the *r* slightly trilled and drawn out): Homemade ginger beer. The name comes from *gemmer*, the Afrikaans word for ginger.

Gogo: Grandmother, in both Xhosa and Zulu

Ma: The formal way married women are addressed, equivalent to *Mrs.*

mgqusho [m(click)OO-shoo] (In Xhosa, *gq* is pronounced as a hard popping sound or click made by pulling the tongue back from the front of the palette): A traditional Xhosa dish made of stamped corn and beans

"Nkosi sikelel' iAfrika" [n-KOH-see see-keh-LEH-lee AH-free-kah]: "God Save Africa"

Tata: A respectful term for fathers or elderly people. In South Africa, young people never address elders by their names only.

Thembi [TEM-bee]: Diminutive for girl's name Thembisa (Xhosa) or Thembisile (Zulu)

toyi-toyi [TOY-ee TOY-ee]: A rhythmic hopping movement usually done by young people at political rallies, protest marches, celebrations, and funerals

My *gogo* is very, very old. When I ask her how old she is, she says, "I am older than this township. When I was born, there were no cars or airplanes." When I ask her if she is older than Tata Nelson Mandela, she laughs and says, "Mandela is a young man compared to me!"

When I come home from school, my mother and father are still at work, so Gogo takes care of me. Gogo calls me her little tail because I follow her everywhere. She lets me carry her beautiful blue cloth bag, in which she keeps her important things. Sometimes she tells me to open it, and I find sweets inside. When my front teeth fell out, she put them in the bag. The next morning she told me to look inside. My teeth had disappeared! Instead there was a two-rand coin inside. I took the money and bought a pair of pink earrings.

Because she was born in the olden days, Gogo knows a lot of things that happened long ago. She tells me many stories that her *gogo* told her about how our ancestors lived before the white people came. She also tells me about the place where our family came from and how we are all related to each other.

One day my father and mother came home very excited because all the main political parties had agreed to the election dates for a new government. Father explained that April 26, 1994, would be a special voting day for old people and those who were very sick. Everyone else would vote on April 27 and 28.

Those two days would be
holidays, and people would not
have to go to work.

"Good, I will vote with the other
old people on April 26," announced Gogo.

We were all shocked when Gogo said this, because she never goes out of the yard. The last time Gogo went out, it was a long time ago, even before I started school. It was when my father took her to the pensions office. When they came back, Gogo was very sick and Father was very angry. He told Mother how they'd had to stand in a long line of people for many hours and the man at the office had shouted at Gogo.

When she heard this story, Mother cried. "They should not treat our elders like that," she said. After that Gogo stayed in her room for many days. My heart was sore because Mother would not let me go into her room. "Gogo cannot tell you any stories because she is very sick," she would say.

Gogo is better now, but she never goes out of the yard anymore. She will not even go to church. The priest has to come to our house to pray with her.

That is why we were so surprised when Gogo said she wanted to vote. "We cannot take you to vote on April 26 because we will be at work," said Father.

"Then I will vote with you on the 27th," said Gogo.

"How will you go to the polling booth?" Father asked Gogo.

"The same way you will go there," replied Gogo.

"But we are going by bus. We cannot have you traveling on a crowded bus! The buses may even be too full on that day, and we may have to walk."

"Besides," said Mother, "there will be long lines of people at the polling station. You will not be able to stand in the lines!"

Mother and Father asked my uncles and aunts to help them try to tell Gogo she could not go to vote. But Gogo refused to listen.

"You want me to die not having voted?" she asked.

Our neighbor Ma Mlambo came to the fence to ask why all the family was gathered at our house. While Father and

Mother were talking to her, I asked Gogo why she wanted to vote so much. I was worried something bad would happen, like the time she went to the pensions office. Gogo told me, "Thembi, black people in South Africa have fought for many years for the right to vote. This is the first time we have a chance to vote for our own leaders, and it might be my last. That is why I must vote, no matter how many miles I have to walk, no matter how long I have to stand in line!"

Ma Mlambo told her uncle, Mr. Ramushu, a rich man who owns many shops in the township, about Gogo. Mr. Ramushu sent a message to Father saying that he would send his own car and driver to take Gogo to vote. I asked Mother and Father if I could come along. At first they said I was too little, but Gogo told them that I must be there to help carry her blue bag. Soon it was time for the elections. The night before, we were all so excited, we couldn't sleep!

Early on the morning of April 27, we dressed in our best clothes. We were waiting eagerly when Mr. Ramushu's big shiny car stopped in front of our small house. As we helped Gogo to the car, all our neighbors came out onto the street. They were cheering. The driver opened the car door for us. My friends shouted, "Look at Thembi in a Benz!" I pretended not to see them. I looked straight in front. I was going to help Gogo to vote. I had no time to laugh and talk to them.

There were many people lined up to vote at the polling booth. The crowd had to move to let the car go through. Mr. Ramushu had told the voting people about Gogo, so they were waiting for her. They said she should not stand in line. A woman called the presiding officer guided us into the voting office.

Gogo showed her identity book to the voting officers. They then put Gogo's hands under a machine. I asked them what it was for.

"It is an ultraviolet machine," explained the presiding officer. "It is against the law to vote twice. This machine helps us make sure that each person votes only once. Look at your *gogo's* hands through the glass in front. You cannot see anything on her hands. Now when we put this colorless liquid on Gogo's hands and put them under the machine for a second time, what do you see?"

"Her hands look blue! Why is that?" I asked.

"Because that liquid is invisible ink. You can see it only under the machine. It cannot be washed off and will fade away only after three days. By that time, the elections will be over."

"So if Gogo tries to vote at another polling booth in the next three days," I said, "her hands will show blue under the machine and they will know that she has already voted! So that's how you tell!"

They then gave Gogo a ballot paper to take into the voting booth. I wanted to cry when they told me I could not go with Gogo into the voting booth. But Gogo hugged me and said, "Thembi, please hold my bag for me while I vote."

"Why can't I go with Gogo?" I asked.

"Because no one should know who she is voting for," the officer said.

"But I already know who she is voting for!" I said.

"Shhh! It is a secret ballot! That means you must not tell anyone!" they said. Mother told me to stop asking so many questions. The voting officers laughed and said I have to ask questions so I will be prepared to vote by the time I am eighteen years old.

When Gogo came out of the voting booth, she put her ballot paper into a big box with an opening on top, like a money box. Some people with big cameras that flash bright lights took pictures of her. Then they took a picture of Gogo and me together! Gogo looked tired, but she smiled and held my hand tightly.

All the people in the room stood up and clapped for a long time. Mother told me they were clapping for Gogo because she was the oldest voter in our township. Mother and Father were crying. I cried, too. I don't know why, because I was very happy.

When we got home in Mr. Ramushu's beautiful car, our yard was full of neighbors and relatives. My aunt Sophie had cooked *mgqusho*, and Ma Mlambo brought a huge pail of *gemmer*. While we were eating, some of my uncles argued about who would win the elections. They became quite angry because they had voted for different parties.

"Be silent!" Father told them. "Let us not worry about that now. The important thing is that we can vote, and Gogo has led the way!"

Everyone began to sing freedom songs and dance. They danced so much, no one remembered to send me to bed. I danced the *toyi-toyi* with my older cousins until our feet were sore. When we were too tired to go on, we all sang our national anthem, "*Nkosi sikelel' iAfrika,*" and crawled into our beds.

The next day there was a picture of Gogo and me in the newspaper. My cousins read aloud the words above the picture: "The past and the future: hundred-year-old voter Mrs. M. Mokoena accompanied by six-year-old great-granddaughter, Thembi." We felt very proud and important!

The whole township celebrated after the elections. When
Mr. Nelson Mandela became president of the country, people
danced and sang in the streets all day and all night. There
were many parties, and we all enjoyed ourselves, but for me
the best day was when Gogo went to vote.